Goal!

ries

First published in 2009
by Wayland

This paperback edition published in 2010 by Wayland

Text copyright © Anna Matthew
Illustration copyright © Heather Heyworth

Wayland
338 Euston Road
London NW1 3BH

Wayland Australia
Level 17/207 Kent Street
Sydney, NSW 2000

Series Editor: Louise John
Editor: Katie Powell
Cover design: Paul Cherrill
Design: D.R.ink
Consultant: Shirley Bickler

A CIP catalogue record for this book is available from the British Library.

ISBN 9780750259255 (hbk)
ISBN 9780750260312 (pbk)

Printed in China

Wayland is a division of Hachette Children's Books,
an Hachette UK Company

www.hachette.co.uk

Goal!

Written by Anna Matthew
Illustrated by Heather Heyworth

WAYLAND

Tom and Dad liked to play football.

Tom liked to get the ball in the net.

Tom kicked the ball.
It hit a bench.

"Sorry. Can I have my
ball, please?" said Tom.

Tom kicked the ball.
It hit a pram.

"Sorry!" said Tom.

Tom kicked the ball up, up, up.

"Oh, no!" said Tom.

The ball went into a bin.

"Sorry," said Dad. "Can I have the ball, please?"

13

Tom kicked the ball.
It went into a van.

"I am sorry," said Tom.

"Look at the ball.
Look at the net.
Kick the ball in the net,"
said Dad.

Tom kicked the ball.

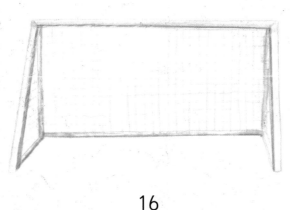

The ball hit the bench,
and the pram,
and the bin,
and the van,
and the tree...

...and it went into the net.

"**Goal!**" said Tom.

Guiding a First Read of
Goal!

It is important to talk through the book with the child before they read it alone. This prepares them for the way the story unfolds, and allows them to enjoy the pictures as you both talk naturally, using the language they will later encounter when reading. Read them the brief overview below, and then follow the suggestions:

1. Talking through the book

Tom liked to score goals, but when he kicked the ball, it hit all sorts of other things in the park. Then Dad showed him how to get the ball into the net.

Let's read the title: **Goal!**
Let's see what happened when Tom kicked the ball. Look. Here he is with Dad on page 4.
Now turn over. Oh no! The ball hit the bench.
"Sorry. Can I have my ball, please?" said Tom.

Continue through the book, guiding the discussion to fit the text, as the child looks at the illustrations.

On page 16, Dad showed Tom how to look and then kick.
Did that work?

Let's see what the ball hit on page 19.
Did he score a goal?
He looks very happy, doesn't he?

2. A first reading of the book

Ask the child to read the book independently, pointing carefully under each word (tracking) while thinking about the story. Praise attempts by the child to correct themselves, and prompt them to use their letter knowledge, the punctuation and check the meaning, for example:

> You said, "Tom liked to go the ball in the net."
> Does that make sense?
> Good. You tried again and sounded 'g...e...t'.
> Does that make sense now?
>
> Well done. You made Tom sound really sorry and polite. I like the way you checked carefully and read it again.

3. Follow-up activities

The high frequency words in this title are:

a am and at can Dad get have I in it liked look my no play said the to up went

- Select two high frequency words, and ask the child or group to find them throughout the book. Discuss the shape of the letters and the letter sounds.
- To memorise the words, ask the child to write them in the air, then write them repeatedly on a whiteboard or on paper, leaving a space between each attempt.

4. Encourage

- Reading the book again – with expression.
- Drawing a picture based on the story.
- Writing one or two sentences using the practised words.

START READING is a series of highly enjoyable books for beginner readers. **The books have been carefully graded to match the Book Bands widely used in schools.** This enables readers to be sure they choose books that match their own reading ability.

Look out for the Band colour on the book in our Start Reading logo.

The Bands are:

	Pink Band 1A & 1B
	Red Band 2
	Yellow Band 3
	Blue Band 4
	Green Band 5
	Orange Band 6
	Turquoise Band 7
	Purple Band 8
	Gold Band 9

START READING books can be read independently or shared with an adult. They promote the enjoyment of reading through satisfying stories supported by fun illustrations.

Anna Matthew loves writing stories about when she was a child. She lived in a seaside town and spent lots of time playing on the beach, and in the park and street. Now her two children are growing up, and she can write about their fun and games, too!

Heather Heyworth lives in Suffolk with her husband, two children and a very demanding cat called Wooster!